One, Two, Guess Who?

For C, with all my love, J

First published in hardback in Great Britain by HarperCollins Publishers in 2000
First published in paperback by Collins Picture Books in 2001
1 3 5 7 9 10 8 6 4 2
ISBN: 0 00 136118 X

Collins Picture Books is an imprint of the Children's Division, part of HarperCollins Publishers Ltd.
Text and illustration copyright © Colin and Jacqui Hawkins 2000
The authors assert the moral right to be identified as the authors of the work.
A CIP catalogue record for this title is available from the British Library.
The HarperCollins website address is: www.fireandwater.com
Manufactured in China

One, Two, Guess Who?

Colin and Jacqui Hawkins

Collins

An imprint of HarperCollinsPublishers

One, Two, What a to-do!
"We'll lock you out," the Little Pigs shout.

Who blew down
the house of twigs,
and frightened away
the Three Little Pigs?

Was it?

Puss in Boots

Big Bad Wolf

The Beast

Three, Four, "What a chore!"
sighs poor Cinders as she scrubs the floor.

Who found the slipper
left behind on the stairs?
The Ugly Sisters
said it was theirs.

Was it?

Tom Thumb

Dick Whittington

Prince Charming

Five, Six, Fiddlesticks!

Red Riding Hood trips up in the wood.

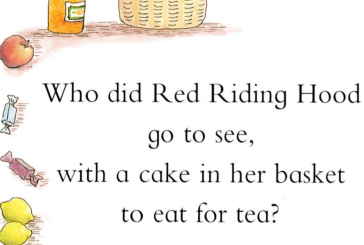

Who did Red Riding Hood
go to see,
with a cake in her basket
to eat for tea?

Was it?

The Wicked Queen

The Fairy Godmother

Granny

Seven, Eight, Through the gate.

The bears leave the porridge to cool on the plate.

When the porridge
wasn't too hot,
who sneaked in
and ate the lot?

Was it?

Hansel & Gretel

Goldilocks

Little Red Riding Hood

Nine, Ten, A magic hen!

"What luck," says Jack, "I'll come again."

9 ▭ ▭ ▭ ▭ ▭ ▭ ▭ ▭ ▭   10 🐔🐔🐔🐔🐔🐔🐔🐔🐔🐔

When Jack climbed the beanstalk into a cloud, who shouted, "Fee, Fi, Fo, Fum," very, very loud?

Was it?

The Troll

Wicked Witch

The Giant

One more time let's say the rhyme

One, Two

What a to-do

Three, Four

Scrub the floor

Five, Six

Fiddlesticks

Seven, Eight

Through the gate

Nine, Ten

A magic hen

One, Two, Three, count with me

Also by Colin and Jacqui Hawkins
Whose House?

Turn the pages, read the clues
And try to guess whose house is whose!

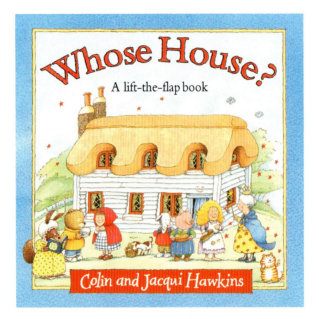

All your favourite nursery rhyme characters invite you to their houses.
Can you work out who lives where?

Winner of the *Parents Play and Learn Gold Award*